This book belongs to...

Puss in Boots

There was once a miller who had three sons. When he died, he left his mill to the eldest son, his cottage to his middle son and only his pet cat to his youngest son, William.

William went and sat under a tree, feeling very miserable and sorry for himself. "What will become of us, Puss?" he moaned.

To William's utter amazement, Puss answered him. "Don't worry, Master," said the cat. "Just do what I say and you will be far richer than either of your brothers!"

Puss told William to get him a fine suit of clothes, a pair of soft leather boots and a strong canvas sack. Then he caught a huge rabbit, put it in the sack, and took it to the palace.

No one there had ever seen a talking cat before, so he was granted an immediate audience with the king.

"Your Majesty," said Puss, "this fine rabbit is a gift from my master, the Marquis of Carabas."

The king had never heard of the Marquis of Carabas, but he was too embarrassed to admit this. "Please thank the Marquis," he said to Puss, "and give him my regards."

The next day, Puss caught some plump partridges and once more he took them to the king, with the same message: "These are from my master."

For several months, Puss went on bringing the king fine gifts.

One day, he heard that the king would be riding along the river bank that afternoon with the princess.

"Master," said Puss, "you must go swimming in the river today."

"Why?" asked William.

"Just do as I say, and you will see," answered Puss.

While William was swimming, Puss hid all his clothes. Then, when he saw the king's carriage approaching, he ran up to it shouting for help. "Help!" cried Puss. "Robbers have stolen my master's clothes!"

When the king recognised the cat, he immediately called to his chief steward and ordered him to bring a fine new suit from the palace.

"It must be of the finest cut," said the king, "and made from the softest cloth, do you hear! Only the best will do for the Marquis of Carabas!"

Once he was dressed in his fine new suit, William looked quite handsome. The princess invited him to join her and her father in the carriage.

As William and the princess sat side by side, they began to fall in love.

Meanwhile, Puss ran ahead until he came to a meadow where he saw some men mowing. "The king's carriage is coming," Puss told them. "When he asks whose meadow this is, say it belongs to the Marquis of Carabas - or you will have your heads cut off!"

The mowers didn't dare to disobey.

When the royal carriage came by, the king asked who the meadow belonged to. The mowers quickly replied, "The Marquis of Carabas."

"I can see that you are very well off indeed," the king said to William, who blushed modestly. That made the princess love him even more!

Down the road, Puss came to a field where men were harvesting corn.

"When the king asks whose corn this is," Puss told them, "say it belongs to the Marquis of Carabas - or you will have your heads cut off!"

The harvesters didn't dare to disobey.

Next, Puss came to an enormous castle which he knew belonged to a fierce ogre. Still he bravely knocked on the door.

When the ogre let him in, Puss bowed low and said, "I have heard that you have wondrous powers, and can change yourself into anything - even a lion or an elephant."

"That is true," said the ogre. And to prove it, he changed himself into a snarling, growling lion.

Puss was terrified and leapt up onto a cupboard. Then the ogre changed himself back again.

"That was amazing," Puss remarked. "But surely it cannot be too difficult for someone of your size to change into a creature as big as a lion. If you were truly the magician they say you are, you could turn into something tiny - like a mouse."

"Of course I can do that!" bellowed the ogre. In an instant he became a little brown mouse scurrying across the floor.

Quick as a flash, Puss leapt off the cupboard, pounced on the mouse and ate it in one big gulp!

Soon, Puss heard the king's carriage drawing near and rushed outside. As it approached, he bowed low and said, "Welcome, Your Majesty, to the home of the Marquis of Carabas."

The king was very impressed indeed. "May we come in?" he asked William.

"Of course, Your Majesty," replied William, a little confused.

As they walked through the castle, the King was delighted to see treasures of great value everywhere he looked. He was so pleased that he said to William, "You are the perfect husband for my daughter."

William and the princess were very happy and later that day they were married. They lived in the ogre's castle happily ever after. Puss, of course, lived with them - though he never chased mice again!